SUPPANDI
TICKLING THE FUNNY BONE

A painter, a driver, a copywriter, and even a chef, Suppandi has applied his truly unique wit to almost every imaginable job out there. The perpetual optimist, Suppandi is never afraid to take up a new occupation, much to the amusement of his fans everywhere. Suppandi has remained, from the day of the character's conception, *Tinkle's* most popular toon.

Based on Tamil folklore about a character called Chappandi, Suppandi was first drawn by the legendary Ram Waeerkar. His daughter, Archana Amberkar, took over after he passed away. She gave the character a more youthful look. In this collection, we have put together some of our favourite Suppandi stories which are illustrated by both, Ram Waeerkar and Archana Amberkar. In them, Suppandi has the challenge of figuring out a number of different tasks and working on a great many jobs.

Suppandi has a resume that is long enough to fill an entire book. We came up with this collection keeping that thought in mind—we hope you love it.

"Suppandi's antics always bring forth a smile. In fact, Suppandi's stories were all I could understand back when I was eight years old. We even enacted a play based on his stories. Now, I'm 17 and Suppandi is still my favourite toon."
– **Holyna Annie Gifta,** *Pondicherry*

"Suppandi, you're the best! *Tinkle's* iconic writers have a great sense of humour and that has made Suppandi more interesting. Suppandi is my favourite toon."
– **Shivom Ghai,** *via email*

"One day, I was reading a Suppandi story and I started to laugh so hard that I hit my mother's table and ended up breaking my mother's expensive makeup box."
– **Tiameren Longkumer,** *via email*

"I like reading and I've been reading Tinkle since a year. All the characters are great but I think Suppandi is the funniest of the lot."
– **Khushi Paliwal,** *via email*

"Suppandi is cool and a lovable fellow. Getting fired from jobs does not make him mellow."
– **Meghna Kamath,** *Pune*

"Before reading the entire comic from cover to cover, I open the magazine and read the Suppandi story first. I love Suppandi; he's my favourite *Tinkle* toon."
– **Shivang Chawla,** *New Delhi*

SUPPANDI ROCKS!

LOOKING FOR A POLICEMAN

SUPPANDI'S NEW EMPLOYER WAS A SMUGGLER. ONE NIGHT –

SUPPANDI, OUR GOODS WILL BE HERE SOON.

GO OUT AND SEE IF THERE ARE ANY POLICEMEN AROUND!

YES, BOSS!

AH! MY GOODS HAVE COME. BUT WHERE IS SUPPANDI?

SUPPANDI! SUPPANDI!! SUPPANDI!!!

HERE I COME!

DID YOU SEE ANY POLICEMEN AROUND?

NOT ONE IN SIGHT!

SO I WENT TO THE POLICE STATION AND CALLED THE INSPECTOR SAHIB.

MELTING POINT

SUPPANDI! GET ME A KILO OF SUGAR FROM THE MARKET.

YES, SIR.

ONE KILO OF SUGAR, PLEASE.

THERE.

OH OH! IT'S STARTING TO RAIN.

HEY, SUPPANDI. DON'T YOU HAVE AN UMBRELLA? THAT SUGAR'LL MELT IF IT GETS WET!

IT WILL?

CAN YOU LEND ME YOUR UMBRELLA, RAMU? I DON'T HAVE ONE RIGHT NOW.

NO WAY! I NEED MINE. WHY DON'T YOU RUN HOME AND GET YOURS?

I'LL DO THAT, SETHJI, PLEASE KEEP THIS PACKET WITH YOU – I'LL GO FETCH MY UMBRELLA.

HEY, SUPPANDI! WHY DON'T YOU UMFURL THAT UMBRELLA SO THAT YOU DON'T GET WET?

IT'S FOR THE SUGAR, RAMU. I WON'T MELT IF I GET WET.

THE CLEAN SWEEP

A SPOONFOOL OF MEDICINE

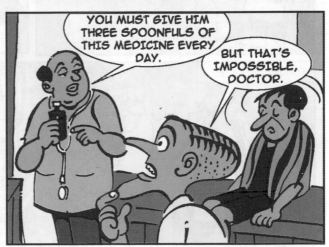

SUPPANDi: Easy Pickings

Story
Sanat Kumar Senapati

Script
Paroma Bose

Pencils & Inks
Archana Amberkar

Colours
B. Meenakshi

Letters
Prasad Sawant

C-R-U-N-C-H

(CRUNCH!) (MUNCH!)

SUPPANDI! DON'T MAKE NOISES WHILE EATING...

...IT IS BAD MANNERS.

YES, SIR.

NEXT DAY –

SUPPANDI! FRY SOME PAPPADS FOR LUNCH.

YES, SIR.

AT LUNCH TIME –

SUPPANDI! WHY ARE THESE PAPPADS SOGGY?

EATING CRISP PAPPADS MAKES A LOT OF NOISE, WHICH YOU SAID WAS BAD MANNERS...

...SO I DIPPED ALL THE FRIED PAPPADS IN WATER!!

AWK!

NO WASTAGE

SUPPANDI'S NEW EMPLOYER WAS A MISER.

SUPPANDI, I AM GOING OUT FOR THE FULL DAY. SEE THAT THE DOG DOESN'T WASTE ITS FOOD.

YES, SIR.

WASTE NOT, WANT NOT!

SIR, FOOD FOR THE AFTERNOON.

AH! THANK YOU, SUPPANDI.

THAT NIGHT –

SUPPANDI, DID THE DOG EAT ALL HIS FOOD?

NO, SIR.

THEN WHAT DID YOU DO WITH THE LEFTOVER RICE?

I MIXED IT WITH CURRY AND...

...PACKED IT FOR YOUR AFTERNOON MEAL!

YECH!

CATCHING A THIEF

ONE DAY –

INSPECTOR, INSPECTOR, HURRY UP! I HAVE CAUGHT A THIEF.

THE POLICE RUSHED TO SUPPANDI'S HOUSE –

WOOOOO

WHERE'S THE THIEF?

HE WAS RIGHT HERE. I DON'T KNOW HOW HE ESCAPED.

YOU TOLD US YOU TIED HIM UP!

I TIED HIS LEGS...

BUT NOT HIS HANDS. HE HAS RUN AWAY ON HIS HANDS!

AARGH!

OBEDIENCE

SUPPANDI'S NEW EMPLOYER WAS A FARMER. ONE MORNING –

SUPPANDI, I AM NOT FEELING WELL.

LOAD THE VEGETABLES ON THE CART, TAKE THEM TO THE MARKET AND SELL THEM.

YES, SIR!

I CAN NEVER BE SURE IF THAT BOY HAS GOT IT RIGHT!

PLEASE REPEAT MY INSTRUCTIONS, SUPPANDI.

I MUST GO TO THE MARKET AND SELL THE VEGETABLES.

GOOD! NOW YOU MAY GO!

BUT SUPPANDI RETURNED IN THE EVENING WITHOUT HAVING SOLD ANYTHING.

WHY DIDN'T YOU SELL THE VEGETABLES?

BECAUSE I COULDN'T REACH THE MARKET!

THE WHEEL OF THE CART GOT STUCK IN THE MUD AND I HAD A TERRIBLE TIME GETTING THE CART UNSTUCK.

AND TO TOP IT ALL THERE WERE SOME TRADERS PESTERING ME TO SELL THEM THE VEGETABLES.

THEN WHY DIDN'T YOU SELL!?

YOU SEEM TO HAVE FORGOTTEN YOUR OWN INSTRUCTIONS, SIR! DIDN'T YOU TELL ME THAT IT WAS IN THE MARKET THAT I WAS TO SELL THEM?

HOW TO HIDE

ICE WISE

ONE HOT SUMMER'S DAY –

WHY ARE YOU PUTTING ICE CUBES IN THE WATER, SIR?

ICE CUBES COOL THE WATER!

REALLY?

THE NEXT DAY –

IT IS VERY WARM. THE HEAT IS INTOLERABLE.

WHAT ARE YOU DOING?

THE ICE CUBES WILL COOL YOU DOWN, SIR.

AARGH

DRIVE-IN RESTAURANT

REMOTE CONTROLLED

SUPPANDI, THIS IS A REMOTE CONTROL.

YES, MA'AM. BUT WHAT IS IT USED FOR?

IT IS USED TO CHANGE CHANNELS ON THE T.V., TO LOWER OR INCREASE THE VOLUME....

OH, I SEE.

LATER -

WAAH WAAH

SSHH! QUIET! AH! AH! COOCHEY... COOCHEY...

WAAH! WAAH!!

SUPPANDI, WHAT ARE YOU DOING?

VOLUME

I'M TRYING TO QUIETEN THE BABY, BUT THE REMOTE DOES NOT SEEM TO WORK.

!

SQUEEZED DRY

SUPPANDI, WHY IS WATER DRIPPING FROM THESE CLOTHES?

BECAUSE I JUST WASHED THEM, SIR.

YOU MUST ALWAYS SQUEEZE OUT THE WATER FROM THE CLOTHES BEFORE HANGING THEM UP. THAT WAY THEY WILL DRY FASTER.

ALL RIGHT, SIR!

NEXT MORNING –

SUPPANDI, RUN DOWN TO THE NEWSSTAND AND GET ME THE MORNING PAPER.

YES, SIR!

DRAT! IT HAS STARTED RAINING.

SUPPANDI, WHEN DID YOU GET BACK FROM THE MARKET? DIDN'T YOU GET THE PAPER?

I DID, SIR. BUT IT GOT WET IN THE RAIN...

...SO I SQUEEZED OUT THE WATER FROM IT AND HUNG IT TO DRY.

BETTER QUALITY

ONCE –

I BOUGHT THIS PAIR OF SHOES A WEEK AGO. THEY'RE ALREADY COMING APART.

SUPPANDI, DON'T GO IN FOR CHEAP THINGS. ALWAYS BUY EXPENSIVE THINGS...

...BECAUSE THE MORE THE PRICE THE BETTER THE QUALITY.

I'LL REMEMBER THAT, SIR.

NOW, GO TO THE MARKET AND GET A KILO OF SUGAR.

RIGHT AWAY, SIR.

LATER –

SUPPANDI, DID YOU GET THE SUGAR?

NO, SIR I'LL BUY IT TOMORROW.

WHY!?

THE PRICE OF SUGAR IS GOING UP TOMORROW...

...AND IF THE PRICE IS MORE THE QUALITY WILL SURELY BE BETTER.

UNPUNCTUAL

SUPPANDI'S NEW EMPLOYER WAS A STICKLER FOR PUNCTUALITY.

SUPPANDI! I TOLD YOU TO COME IN TO WORK AT 9 A.M. SHARP. IT'S THREE MINUTES PAST NINE...

...DON'T WALK IN LATE AGAIN.

YES, SIR.

NEXT DAY –

SUPPANDI! WHY ARE YOU CRAWLING ON ALL FOURS?

I WAS ONLY FOLLOWING YOUR INSTRUCTIONS, SIR. IT IS FIVE PAST NINE...

...AND YOU SAID I WAS NEVER TO WALK IN LATE AGAIN!

AAARGH!

THE VANISHING RICE

SUPPANDI'S EMPLOYER HAD BOUGHT A VACUUM CLEANER —

WHAT IS IT USED FOR?

IT SUCKS IN DUST AND HELPS IN CLEANING.

SUPPANDI, MAKE FRIED RICE TODAY. BUT REMEMBER TO CLEAN THE RICE PROPERLY.

YES, SIR.

LATER —

WHERE IS THE FRIED RICE, SUPPANDI?

THERE'S NO RICE, SIR.

WHAT DO YOU MEAN?

IT VANISHED WHEN I CLEANED IT...

...WITH THE VACUUM CLEANER.

!

20

FOLLOWING INSTRUCTIONS

GOOD MANNERS

SIX FAST LEGS

RAISING MONEY

HALF IS GOOD

BOILING

SUPPANDI, COOK SOME MACARONI FOR LUNCH.

YES, SIR.

SHORTLY –

SIR, THE MACARONI IS BECOMING BIGGER AND LONGER.

OH GOD! WHAT A FOOL!

IT IS BUT NATURAL, SUPPANDI. SOLIDS EXPAND ON HEATING.

LATER –

SUPPANDI, WHAT ARE YOU DOING?

I'M BOILING MY OLD CLOTHES. THEY DON'T FIT ME ANYMORE.

SINCE SOLIDS EXPAND ON HEATING, I HOPE THEY'LL BECOME BIGGER.

!

GOING IN CIRCLES

A NEWCOMER TO THE TOWN WAS LOST. UNFORTUNATELY, HE MET SUPPANDI.

EX...EXCUSE ME, DO YOU KNOW WHERE THE POST OFFICE IS?

YES.

WELL...ER... WHERE IS IT?

OH, IT'S RIGHT OPPOSITE MY HOUSE.

AND WHERE'S YOUR HOUSE?

OPPOSITE THE POST OFFICE.

SHEESH! AND WHERE ARE YOUR HOUSE AND THE POST OFFICE?

THEY'RE...

...OPPOSITE EACH OTHER.

GURK!

SUPER PANDI
MONITOR MENACE

Story, Pencils & Inks
Savio Mascarenhas

Script
Sean D'mello

Colours
Snehangshu Mazumder

Letters
Pranay Bendre

HELLO, THIS IS MADDY COMPUTER CARE. HOW MAY WE BE OF ASSISTANCE TODAY?

I'M SO PROUD OF MADDY. HE'S STARTED HIS OWN COMPUTER COMPANY.

MADDY COMPUTER CARE

IT WAS NICE OF HIM TO LET ME WORK HERE WHILE I LOOK FOR A NEW JOB.

SUPPANDI, I NEED YOU TO GO AND COLLECT A MONITOR, OKAY? THIS LADY HAS BEEN BUGGING ME SINCE FOREVER TO COME AND TAKE IT.

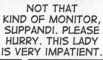

SURE, MADDY. BUT WHAT DO YOU WANT WITH A CLASSROOM MONITOR ANYWAY?

NOT THAT KIND OF MONITOR, SUPPANDI. PLEASE HURRY. THIS LADY IS VERY IMPATIENT.

SOMETIME LATER...

HELLO MA'AM, I'M FROM MADDY COMPUTER CARE.

FINALLY! THE MONITOR IS IN THE GARAGE. I HAVEN'T BEEN INSIDE IN YEARS. IT'S FULL OF LIZARDS. I'M LEAVING YOU TO DEAL WITH THEM.

IT'S REALLY DARK INSIDE. I WONDER IF THERE'S A LIGHT...

creeeeaaak

YOU WILL NOT STAND IN MY WAY, YOU MONSTER! I WILL HAVE THAT MONITOR.

FOOLED!

ONCE AT LUNCH –

YECH! THERE ARE SO MANY FLIES IN THE ROOM.

THEY SEEM TO KNOW WHEN IT IS OUR LUNCH TIME. THEY ARE HERE AT ONE O'CLOCK EVERY DAY.

NEXT DAY –

SIR, LUNCH IS SERVED.

WHY HAVE YOU SERVED LUNCH SO EARLY? IT'S ONLY 12 O'CLOCK.

I HAVE OUTSMARTED THE FLIES, MADAM...

...THEY'LL COME FOR LUNCH AT ONE O'CLOCK. WE'LL HAVE FINISHED EATING BY THEN.

GROAN!

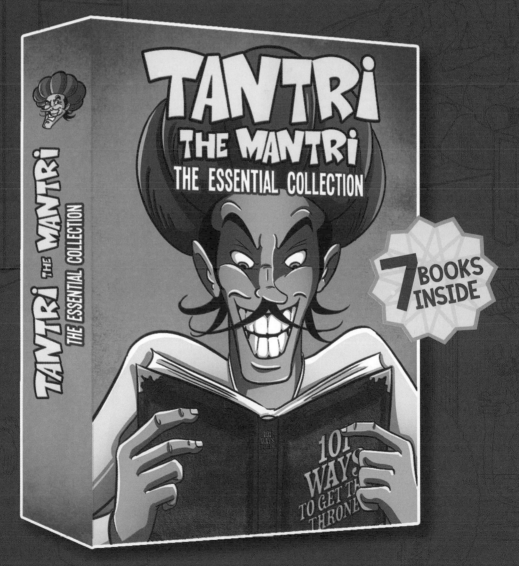

Meet the Artist

Ram Waeerkar

The stories that you have read so far have been illustrated by the legendary Ram Waeerkar. Ram Waeerkar was one of the pioneers of Indian Comics. It was he who gave Suppandi his iconic look—a long, sharp nose, a square jaw and the few strands of hair—in 1983 when the character debuted in *Tinkle*. Suppandi has since then become the poster boy of Indian comics and a childhood friend of thousands.

Ram Waeerkar also gave form to several other *Tinkle* characters such as Pyarelal and folk toons such as Nasruddin Hodja. He has illustrated about 90 *Amar Chitra Katha* titles!

His drawings are characterized by bold and versatile strokes that impart vigour and liveliness to the characters he illustrates.

Archana Amberkar

The stories that you will read henceforth have been illustrated by Ram Waeerkar's daughter, Archana Amberkar. Archana took over drawing Suppandi sometime around 2003. She has added her own style while illustrating Suppandi, giving him a more youthful and modern look. Archana experiments with different looks for Suppandi and has the most fun drawing him.

Archana Amberkar is also the artist of many other *Tinkle* toons such as Pyarelal, Ina Mina Mynah Mo, and Kalia the Crow. Her illustrations are adorable, cute and continue to make readers smile.

Suppandi
Curtains

Readers' Choice
Based on an idea by:
Yash Ved,
Mumbai
Illustrations:
Archana Amberkar

SUPPANDI'S EMPLOYER HAD MOVED INTO A NEW HOUSE.

SUPPANDI, WE NEED CURTAINS. COUNT THE NUMBER OF WINDOWS IN THE HOUSE AND GET CURTAINS FOR ALL OF THEM.

LATER —

HAVE YOU BOUGHT THE CURTAINS?

YES, SIR.

GOOD, LET'S PUT THEM UP.

SOON —

WE'VE COVERED ALL THE WINDOWS... BUT THERE ARE TWO LEFT. WHY DID YOU BUY EXTRA CURTAINS?

FOR THE WINDOWS IN THE COMPUTER, SIR!

SHEESH!

34

SUPPANDI
UMBRELLA TO THE RESCUE

Based on a story sent by **elizabethammu** for the **tinkleonline gallery**
Illustrator: Archana Amberkar
Colourist: Umesh Sarode

SUPPANDI AND HIS EMPLOYER HAD GONE SHOPPING, WHEN –

OH, THESE UNSEASONAL RAINS!

WHY DO PEOPLE WITHOUT UMBRELLAS COVER THEIR HEADS INSTEAD OF COVERING THEIR BODIES, SIR?

THAT'S BECAUSE IF YOUR HEAD GETS WET, YOU'LL FALL ILL.

AH, HERE'S A SHOP SELLING UMBRELLAS!

WE'LL BUY TWO UMBRELLAS – ONE FOR YOU AND ONE FOR ME.

BUY ONE FOR THE BATHROOM TOO, SIR.

BATHROOM?

YOU DON'T WANT YOUR HEAD TO GET WET IN THE SHOWER, DO YOU?

At the Dairy

A Suppandi Tale

Story: Carisa Rocha

Script: Rajani Thindiath

Illustrator & Colourist:
Archana Amberkar

SUPPANDI WENT TO WORK AT A DAIRY –

SUPPANDI, TODAY I'LL TEACH YOU HOW TO PREPARE *BASUNDI**. IT IS VERY SIMPLE. YOU JUST HAVE TO KEEP STIRRING THE MILK TILL IT'S REDUCED TO HALF. DO THAT TILL I RETURN.

VERY WELL, SIR.

I'VE BEEN STIRRING FOR AN HOUR AND THERE'S BARELY ANY DIFFERENCE IN THE QUANTITY OF THE MILK!

AHA! I'VE AN IDEA!

HOW'S THE *BASUNDI* COMING ALONG, SUPPANDI?

IT IS READY, SIR!

IT'S READY! IMPOSSIBLE! IT SHOULD HAVE TAKEN ANOTHER HOUR AT LEAST! HOW DID YOU GET IT TO REDUCE **TO HALF** SO FAST?

*SWEET DISH MADE BY BOILING MILK.

EASY! I KEPT DRINKING FROM IT AS I STIRRED!

AWK!

TWO·IN·ONE
A Suppandi Tale

Based on an idea sent by:
Kshitij Birdi, New Delhi.
Script: R. Nalini
Illustrations & Colouring: Archana Amberkar

SUPPANDI'S EMPLOYER HAD TAUGHT HIM HOW TO WRITE A LETTER.

SUPPANDI, HAVE YOU FINISHED WRITING LETTERS TO YOUR MOTHER IN MATHURA AND SISTER IN KOLKATA?

I HAVE JUST STARTED, SIR.

OK, SHOW THEM TO ME WHEN YOU FINISH! AND DON'T WASTE PAPER. WRITE ON BOTH SIDES.

YES, SIR.

AN HOUR LATER –

I'VE FINISHED, SIR.

SUPPANDI, THIS IS JUST ONE LETTER. WHERE'S THE OTHER?

YOU SAID NOT TO WASTE PAPER, SIR. ON ONE SIDE I'VE WRITTEN TO MY MOTHER IN MATHURA…

…AND ON THE OTHER, TO MY SISTER IN KOLKATA!.

SUPPANDI
The Businessman

Illustrations:
Archana Amberkar

Colouring:
Rajesh Phatak

HOW'S BUSINESS, DABBOO?

DULL! MY COMPETITOR IS DOING MUCH BETTER.

YOU SHOULD MAKE A TWO-IN-ONE OFFER LIKE THAT!

I CAN'T AFFORD TO GIVE ONE SANDWICH FREE! I DON'T KNOW HOW HE DOES IT!

BUY ONE SANDWICH, GET ONE FREE!

SO THE PROBLEM IS HOW TO MAKE A TWO-IN-ONE OFFER BUT NOT GIVE ANYTHING FREE. LET ME THINK ABOUT IT!

I'VE SOLVED YOUR PROBLEM, DABBOO! HERE, PUT UP THIS SIGN I'VE PAINTED FOR YOU!

WHAT DOES IT SAY?

READ FOR YOURSELF!

BUY ONE SANDWICH, PAY FOR TWO!!

YO, SUPPANDI!

Script: Margie Sastry
Illustrations: Archana Amberkar
Colouring: Rajesh Phatak

SUPPANDI'S NEWEST EMPLOYER WAS A SOFTWARE ENGINEER FROM THE USA.

WOW!

HERE, TAKE THESE! I'M FED UP OF MY UNIVERSITY STUFF.

SUPPANDI ALSO PICKED UP A NEW VOCABULARY.

YO! AH-HAH! COOL!

YO! COOL!

ONE DAY –

SUPPANDI, GO TO THE Y3K OFFICE AND GIVE THEM THIS CD*. IT'S A COPY OF MY MOST RECENT INVENTION.

YO!

AT THE Y3K OFFICE THE CEO* WAS INSTRUCTING HIS ASSISTANT, SLIMY JOE –

I'M EXPECTING A REVOLUTIONARY GAME DESIGN FROM ONE OF THE BRIGHTEST GUYS IN SILICON VALLEY CALLED SHAWN. IF HE COMES, TREAT HIM WELL.

YES, SIR!

39

*COMPACT DISC
*CHIEF EXECUTIVE OFFICER

SUPPANDI AMBLED INTO THE Y3K OFFICE –

YOU ARE FROM…?

SHAWN, MR SHAWN.

SIR, MR. SHAWN IS HERE TO SEE YOU.

GREAT! I'LL IMPRESS HIM AND CONFIRM MY RAISE. HEH! HEH!

HI, DUDE!

YO!

SLIMY JOE COULD NOT CONTAIN HIS ADMIRATION FOR SUPPANDI –

YOUR HAIR, MAN, IT'S AWESOME! WHAT'S THIS STYLE CALLED?

WHAT ON EARTH IS HE TALKING ABOUT? I HAD BETTER PLAY SAFE.

YO!

SUPPANDI TOOK OUT THE CD.

CHECK THIS.

RIGHT AWAY!

WOW, THIS IS MIND BLOWING! A COMPUTER GAME BASED ON THE DNA DOUBLE HELIX MODEL!

41

*MAKE A COPY OF THE THE CD.

SUPPANDI, THE CHAUFFEUR

Based on an idea by:
Sanjay Dinker,
Chennai.

Script: R. Nalini
Illustrations and Colouring:
Archana Amberkar

SUPPANDI, WE HAVE TO GO TO MY NEW OFFICE IN AARAM NAGAR. DO YOU KNOW THE WAY?

NO, SIR!

UMM...OK, DO AS I SAY! KEEP GOING STRAIGHT FOR...TEN MINUTES AND THEN TAKE A LEFT.

OK, SIR!

...6...7...

...8...9...

SMASH!

WHAT IS WRONG WITH YOU? WHY DID YOU RAM THE CAR INTO THE TREE?

YOU ASKED ME TO GO STRAIGHT FOR 10 MINUTES SIR. I WAS DOING EXACTLY THAT BUT THE TREE WAS IN THE WAY!

suppandi
in *A Fishy Tale*

Writer:
Akshata Shastry

Illustrator & Colourist:
Archana Amberkar

SUPPANDI'S NEW PET WAS CAUSING HIM A LOT OF WORRY...

HEY, SUPPANDI! HOW IS YOUR FISH DOING?

NOT TOO GOOD, NOT TOO GOOD!

SICK, IS IT?

NO, NO, IT'S FINE! IT JUST WON'T WHISTLE OR TALK.

YOU'VE BEEN TRYING TO TEACH IT TO TALK AND WHISTLE? IT'S A FISH, YOU IDIOT!

IT IS YOU WHO IS THE IDIOT!

...SEE, THIS IS A PARROT FISH!

Gadget Woes

A SUPPANDI TALE

Readers' Choice

Based on a story sent by:
Sruthi K., Chennai, Tamil Nadu.

Illustrations: Archana Amberkar

SUPPANDI, BRING DOWN THE MIXER-GRINDER FROM THAT SHELF. I WANT YOU TO GRIND SOME SPICES.

YES, MA'AM.

IT'S NOT WORKING!

HMM...IT HASN'T BEEN USED FOR A WHILE. GADGETS THAT AREN'T USED FREQUENTLY OFTEN STOP WORKING.

REALLY, MA'AM?

YES, WE SHOULD USE THEM REGULARLY TO KEEP THEM IN GOOD WORKING ORDER.

LATER THAT MONTH —

(GASP!) LOOK AT HOW MUCH THE PHONE BILL IS!

SUPPANDI! DO YOU KNOW ANYTHING ABOUT THIS?

OH, YES, MA'AM!

I WANTED TO KEEP THE PHONE IN FINE WORKING ORDER. SO I HAVE BEEN USING IT ALL THE TIME!

GAK!

45

Close Match

A Suppandi Tale

Writer:
Rajani Thindiath

Illustrations:
Archana Amberkar

Colouring:
Umesh Sarode

SUPPANDI, MY HAIR IS FALLING OFF VERY FAST. GET A WIG FROM THE MARKET THAT CLOSELY MATCHES MY HAIR.

YES, SIR.

AH! SO YOU'RE BACK. YOU'VE GOT THE WIG?

HERE IT IS!

HMMM... I LOOK 10 YEARS YOUNGER, EVEN IF I DO SAY SO MYSELF!

THE NEXT MORNING –

SUPPANDI! THE HAIR FROM MY WIG IS FALLING OFF!

I KNOW, SIR! THE SHOPKEEPER TOLD ME THAT HAIR WOULD FALL OUT FROM IT!

THE SHOPKEEPER TOLD YOU? THEN WHY DID YOU BUY IT!

WELL, YOU DID SAY YOU WANTED A WIG THAT CLOSELY MATCHES YOUR OWN HAIR, SIR!

Readers' Choice

Based on an idea sent by:
Bhavna K. Vaidya,
Andheri (W), Mumbai - 400 053.

**Illustrations:
Archana Amberkar**

TIME TROUBLE
A Suppandi Tale

48

SUPPANDI BECOMES RICH

Script:
Luis Fernandes

Illustrations:
Archana Amberkar

SUPPANDI'S NEW EMPLOYER WAS AN EXPLORER.

NOT MUCH FURTHER TO GO NOW....

AH, THERE IT IS! THE CAVE INDICATED IN THE MAP!

WHAT'S IN THE CAVE, SIR?

TREASURE! WE'LL...I MEAN, I'LL BE RICH!

RICH?

I HOPE YOU'LL GIVE ME A RAISE, SIR!

WE'LL SEE, WE'LL SEE!

HOW MUCH SHOULD I ASK FOR? 20 RUPEES? 25?

25 MIGHT BE TOO MUCH.

DARK AND SCARY IN HERE!

A S...SNAKE!

AAAAAAH!

I CAME PREPARED FOR ALL SUCH PROBLEMS.

THIS SMOKE BOMB WILL DRIVE OUT THE SNAKE.

THERE!

IT'S GONE! WE'LL WAIT FOR SOME TIME TILL THE SMOKE DISPERSES.

I THINK WE CAN GO IN NOW.

THERE! THE TREASURE CHEST!

BLUE TO WHITE

A Suppandi tale

Readers' Choice
Based on an idea sent by:

Vishnu V.,
Palakkad - 678 001.

Illustrations:
Archana Amberkar

ONE DAY –

MADAM, WHAT IS THAT?

IT IS LIQUID WHITENER, SUPPANDI. IT IS A BLUE LIQUID THAT MAKES WHITE CLOTHES SPARKLING WHITE.

A FEW DAYS LATER –

YOU MUST BRUSH YOUR TEETH PROPERLY TO MAKE THEM SPARKLING WHITE.

YES, MA.

COME, MUNNU, I WILL HELP YOU MAKE YOUR TEETH WHITE.

?

EEEEE! MA!

WHAT HAPPENED? SUPPANDI, WHY IS MUNNU SHOUTING?

I WAS TRYING TO PERSUADE MUNNU TO BRUSH HIS TEETH WITH THE LIQUID WHITENER. IT WILL MAKE HIS TEETH SPARKLING WHITE, WON'T IT?

AAARGH!

PASSWORD
A Suppandi tale

Script: Luis Fernandes

Illustrations: Archana Amberkar

SUPPANDI'S NEW MASTER WAS A GANGSTER, BUT SUPPANDI DIDN'T KNOW THAT.

ONE DAY—

TAKE THIS PACKET AND STAND AT THE BUS STOP OUTSIDE THE SCHOOL.

A MAN OR POSSIBLY A WOMAN WILL COME AND SAY, 'MARY HAD A LITTLE LAMB'. THAT IS THE PASSWORD.

GIVE THE PACKET TO THAT PERSON.

ALL RIGHT, SIR.

SOME TIME LATER –

BACK SO SOON? DID YOU GIVE THE PACKET?

YES, SIR. YOU WERE EXPECTING A MAN OR WOMAN…

… BUT THE FIRST PERSON TO SAY THE PASSWORD WAS A SCHOOLBOY. HE SAID 'MARY HAD A LITTLE LAMB'…

WHAT!

…AND I GAVE THE PACKET TO HIM.

YOU GAVE THE PACKET OF DIAMONDS TO A SCHOOLBOY?! OH, YOU BLUNDERING FOOL!!

OH, SO THEY WERE DIAMONDS. BUT WHY DOES HE HAVE TO GET SO UPSET? THE MATTER CAN BE EASILY SET RIGHT.

THE PRINCIPAL OF THE SCHOOL WON'T SEE ME, AND THE WATCHMEN WON'T LET ME IN! YOU'VE PUT ME INTO A MESS, YOU NINCOMPOOP!

NOT TO WORRY, SIR. EVERYTHING IS UNDER CONTROL.

I PHONED THE POLICE AND TOLD THEM EVERYTHING. THEY'LL RECOVER THE DIAMONDS FOR YOU.

WHAT!

THEY SEEMED VERY KEEN TO MEET YOU. THERE, I THINK I CAN HEAR THEM COMING!

DRAT!

?!

COME IN! MY EMPLOYER LEFT IN A HURRY THROUGH THE WINDOW BUT I'M SURE HE'LL COME BACK SOON.

THE OIL STAIN
A Suppandi tale

Readers' Choice
Based on an idea sent by
Genito Chophi, Nagaland.

Illustrations:
Archana Amberkar

SIR, I'VE WASHED THIS SHIRT SO MANY TIMES BUT THE STAIN ISN'T GOING.

IT'S AN OIL STAIN, SUPPANDI. IT WON'T GO WITH JUST WATER.

HERE, WASH IT WITH THIS DETERGENT. THAT WILL GET THE OIL OUT.

DETERGENT... RIGHT, SIR.

A WEEK LATER —

SOME OF MY FRIENDS ARE COMING OVER. GO AND BUY SOME SAMOSAS.

YES, SIR.

SOON —

PLEASE HAVE SOME SAMOSAS.

THEY LOOK FUNNY!

THEY TASTE FUNNY....

OH, THEY WERE TOO OILY, SIR.

SO I WASHED THEM WITH WATER AND DETERGENT TO REMOVE THE OIL.

AAARGH!

!!

BIG EARS

A Suppandi Tale

Script :
Luis Fernandes

Illustrations :
Archana Amberkar

SUPPANDI
His and Hers

Readers' Choice
Based on a story sent by
Anmol Puranik
Udupi, Karnataka

Script: R. Nalini

Illustrator:
Archana Amberkar

Colourist:
Umesh Sarode

SUPPANDI, NISHA WANTS ME TO READ HER A STORY EVERY DAY. BUY A STORY BOOK WITH LOTS OF PICTURES...

YES, SIR!

SOON –

SUPPANDI, THIS BOOK SAYS 'STORIES FOR YOUNG BOYS'...

...YOU SHOULD HAVE GOT 'STORIES FOR YOUNG GIRLS' SINCE NISHA IS A GIRL...

NOW GET THIS EXCHANGED... AND, OH...

...NAINA'S SCHOOL STARTS ON MONDAY. I'LL GIVE YOU A LIST OF BOOKS YOU'VE TO GET HER.

YES, SIR! I'LL GO IN THE EVENING.

THAT EVENING –

SUPPANDI, YOU'VE MISSED ONE BOOK FROM THIS LIST...

NO, SIR... I DELIBERATELY DIDN'T BUY IT, BECAUSE NAINA IS A GIRL...

...AND THE TITLE ON THE TEXTBOOK SAID 'HIS-STORY'!

?!

SUPPANDI
ALERT WATCHMAN!

Readers' Choice
Based on an idea by:
Bhavya Chheda
Script: R. Nalini
Illustrator: Archana Amberkar
Colourist: Umesh Sarode

THE SECRETARY OF SHEETAL APARTMENTS WANTED TO HIRE A RELIABLE WATCHMAN. AND HE DID FIND ONE – OUR VERY OWN SUPPANDI !

YOUR JOB IS TO KEEP AN EYE ON THE BUILDING. AND NO SLEEPING ON DUTY, GET IT ?

YES, SIR !

ONE NIGHT –

HOW ARE YOU DOING, SUPPANDI ?

VERY WELL, SIR !

THAK ! THAK !

SUPPANDI !! A THIEF !

LET'S GET HIM... GIVE ME THAT STAFF !

THIEF ! THIEF !...

CATCH HIM...!

THE RESIDENTS RETURNED AFTER HANDING OVER THE THIEF TO THE POLICE –

HOW COULD YOU JUST STAND THERE ! WHY DIDN'T YOU HELP US NAB THE THIEF, SUPPANDI ?

I WOULD HAVE HELPED, SIR... BUT DUTY IS DUTY !

DUTY ?

DIDN'T YOU TELL ME MY JOB WAS TO *WATCH* THE BUILDING ?

61

SKIP A DAY
A Suppandi tale

Idea: Dhiraj V. Chawla
Script: Janaki Viswanathan
Illustrations: Archana Amberkar

FRESH VEGETABLES

A Suppandi Tale

Readers' Choice

Based on story sent by:
R. Rama, Chennai.

Illustrations :
Archana Amberkar

THE HAUNTED HOUSE!

Writer: Luis
Illustrator: Archana Amberkar
Colourist: Rajesh Phatak

SUPPANDI! THE LANDLORD HAS THROWN US OUT OF OUR HOUSE!

WHAT! BUT WHY, MADDY?

ONE REASON IS WE'VE NOT PAID OUR RENT FOR 10 MONTHS!

IS THAT ALL? COME, I'LL TALK TO HIM!

NO, NO, SUPPANDI! THERE'S ANOTHER REASON!

HE SAYS HE CAN'T STAND YOUR IDIOTIC CHATTER ANYMORE!

IDIOTIC CHATTER! WHAT NONSENSE!!

I'VE GIVEN HIM SO MUCH VALUABLE ADVICE HE SHOULD BE GRATEFUL TO ME!!

FORGET IT, SUPPANDI!

COME, LET'S TALK TO HIM!

TO TELL YOU THE TRUTH, I AM FED UP OF YOUR IDIOTIC CHATTER TOO!!

WHAT!

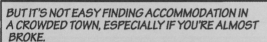

SOON —

HERE IT IS! LOOKS GHOSTLY, DOESN'T IT!

GHOSTS DON'T FRIGHTEN ME! WHAT FRIGHTENS ME IS GETTING WET...

... AND IT'S STARTING TO RAIN!

PLINK

IT'S ONLY A FEW DROPS SUPPANDI!!

GET UNDER SHELTER!

THE DOOR IS LOCKED!

YOU THOUGHT THEY WOULD KEEP IT OPEN FOR US?!

IT'S RAINING HEAVILY NOW! GET INTO THE DOORWAY!!

I'VE NEVER SEEN A GHOST EITHER, BUT IN MY CASE IT'S BECAUSE I HIDE FROM THEM! I NEVER GO WHERE GHOSTS MAY BE MOVING AROUND!

THAT IS WHY I FEEL SO JITTERY HERE!

AH, THIS MUST BE THE BEDROOM! NICE, NICE... TWO BEDS AND A BATHROOM!

THIS IS THE SORT OF BEDROOM THEY SHOW IN HORROR MOVIES! I DON'T THINK I'LL SLEEP A WINK!

AAAH!

W-WHAT'S UP THERE, SUPPANDI? DID YOU SEE SOMETHING!

THE ROOF'S LEAKING! A RAIN DROP FELL ON ME!

YOU SCREAMED FOR THAT! I HOPE THE WHOLE ROOF FALLS ON YOU, YOU MORON!!

SUPPANDI!

WHERE COULD HE HAVE GONE!

SUPPANDI! SUPPANDI!

HE HAS DISAPPEARED! VANISHED INTO THIN AIR!

I TOLD HIM THIS PLACE WAS HAUNTED!

THE VAMPIRES HAVE GOT HIM AND NOW THEY MUST BE CREEPING UP ON ME!

AAAAAEEEEEEEEEEE!!!!!!!!!!

EARLY, THE FOLLOWING MORNING —

SLEPT LIKE A LOG!

THE ONLY TIME I AWOKE WAS WHEN I HEARD MADDY SCREAMING IN HIS SLEEP!! CRAZY FELLOW!!

70

72